How to make your Felicity wishes

W I S H

With this book comes an extra-special wish
for you and your best friend.

Hold the book together at each end and
both close your eyes.

Wriggle your noses and think of a
number under ten.

Open your eyes, whisper the numbers you
thought of to each other.

Add these numbers together. This is your

Magic Number.

you

best friend

Place your little finger
on the stars, and say your magic number
out loud together. Now make your wish
quietly to yourselves. And maybe, one day,
your wish might just come true.

Love felicity x

For Becky, a real fairy godmother,
and for Isabella x

FELICITY WISHES
Felicity Wishes © 2000 Emma Thomson
Licensed by White Lion Publishing

Text and Illustrations © 2007 Emma Thomson

First published in Great Britain in 2007 by Hodder Children's Books

A Catalogue record for this book is available from the British Library.

ISBN: 9 780 34094393 9

Printed in the UK by CPI Bookmarque, Croydon, CR0 4TD

The paper and board used in this paperback by Hodder Children's Books are natural recyclable
products made from wood grown in sustainable forests. The manufacturing processes
conform to the environmental regulations of the country of origin.

Hodder Children's Books
A division of Hachette Children's Books, 338 Euston Road, London NW1 3BH
An Hachette Livre UK Company

Emma Thomson's

felicity Wishes

fairy fame

and other stories

CONTENTS

Mystery Mansion

Felicity Wishes and her friends were sitting in Sparkles, their favourite café, trying to decide what to do. It was the first Saturday in ages that none of them had any plans.

"We could go bowling," Holly suggested.

"I went last weekend," Winnie said.

"How about ice skating?" Felicity proposed. But Polly had heard it was shut for repairs.

"We could go for a walk in the woods," Daisy said dreamily.

"I've lost my walking boots," Felicity replied.

None of the fairies knew what to do.

"Unless..." Winnie began, then paused.

"What?" they all chorused.

"Well, ever since I came to Little Blossoming I've wanted to explore the old mansion over the hill," Winnie told them.

Winnie was talking about an old ruin of a house on the very outskirts of Little Blossoming. The fairies had flown over it hundreds of times but never thought about going inside.

"That old thing! Why would you want to go there?" Holly asked, wrinkling her nose.

"It might be fun!" Winnie replied with an adventurous heart.

Felicity smiled. "I don't see why not. It sounds exciting!"

"Wouldn't it be trespassing?" Polly asked sensibly.

"I don't think so. It's abandoned!" Winnie was almost at the door already.

"Then let's go!" Felicity cried, jumping up from her seat.

"At least we'll be outside in the sunshine," Daisy said, following.

Holly and Polly were far more reluctant to go, but without anything better to do they followed their friends.

It didn't take the fairies long to reach the old house; it was far closer than they had thought. Once they got there, though, they found the old metal gates closed and locked.

"Well that's the end of that," Felicity sighed, turning to go home. "We clearly aren't supposed to go in."

"Ta da!" Winnie had been fiddling with the padlock and now the gates swung wide open.

"What did you do?" Holly asked, amazed.

"Magic!" Winnie laughed. "Well, actually the lock had completely rusted through so it just fell apart in my hand. No one has touched it for years. It must be all right to explore."

The fairies cautiously stepped forward into the most overgrown garden they had ever seen.

"Oh, it's so sad," Daisy said, looking at the ivy and brambles covering everything in sight.

They had to flutter above the ground to avoid getting scratched. When they reached the house, the front door was barely visible behind a blanket of creeping ivy and wild roses. Winnie pulled back as much as she could, discovering that the heavy old door was already wedged open. She led the way inside to a very dark and dusty hallway.

"Wow! It's huge!" Felicity said, marvelling at the high ceiling and

grand staircase in front of her.

"This room alone is bigger than my house!" Daisy said in amazement.

Holly, meanwhile, had wiped the dust and dirt off a wall with her finger to find some beautiful wallpaper with a bright-blue background and gold swirls beneath. "This must have been such a lovely home," she said, sad that it had become so neglected.

"Come on, let's look around," Winnie said, racing up to the staircase. "Oops! Mind the broken step!"

Upstairs were ten bedrooms, all with four-poster beds covered in dust-sheets. Felicity picked up the corner of a sheet to peer underneath, only to find a huge spider!

"Ahhh!" she screamed, jumping back straight into Polly. Polly toppled on to the floor, sending a cloud of dust into the air as she hit the thick rug covering the wooden floorboards.

As Polly got up she saw an intricate pattern of rich colours on the rug where she had unsettled the dust.

"You know, all this needs is a good clean and some tender loving care. I bet it could look as good as new in no time!" she said, looking at the fairies around her.

They all grinned at her, ready to start work straight away!

* * *

The fairies met at eight o'clock the next morning armed with brushes and vacuum cleaners, dusters and polish, floor cleaners, buckets and mops, eager to return to their house. But when they got there the front door was swinging open in the breeze.

"That's funny," Winnie said. "I thought I closed it when we left last night."

They went inside, only to find a fairy sitting on the stairs in the hall.

"Oh, sorry, we, er, thought this place

was deserted," Felicity muttered, feeling very guilty.

"It is!" the fairy replied in a very squeaky voice, almost a whisper.

"I just keep an eye on it and I noticed you all here yesterday. I wanted to say hello because I used to live here."

"We're so sorry, we didn't mean to intrude," Polly said, stepping forward. "We didn't think anyone had lived here for years and we wanted to do it up a bit. We'll go!"

"Oh no, please don't!" the fairy squeaked, looking very disappointed. "I lived here a very long time ago, but it was just too big to look after all on my own. I'd love to help you clean it. I can even tell you what it used to look like!"

Felicity smiled. "It would be wonderful to have your help. I'm Felicity and these are my friends Holly, Polly, Winnie and Daisy," she said, introducing everyone.

"I'm Eliza. It's lovely to meet you all," the squeaky fairy smiled.

As Felicity, Holly, Polly and Eliza cleaned the inside of the house, Daisy and Winnie explored the garden.

"You know, with a good pair of shears and a spade I bet this garden could look great in no time!" Daisy said as she fluttered around.

The fairies worked tirelessly all day and well into the night, by candlelight.

* * *

That week at school passed extremely slowly. The fairies spent every lunchtime in the library, looking through history books. Polly wanted to see what the house would have looked like when it was new. Holly looked at books about interior design, Daisy looked at gardening books. Felicity looked to see what kind of fairies used to live in houses that big and Winnie drew maps of the house, labelling exactly what needed repairing.

By the time the weekend finally arrived they couldn't wait to get started again. Eliza met them in the entrance hall.

Winnie and Daisy stayed outdoors. Winnie abseiled down the walls to check for any damage on the outside of the house and Daisy dug the garden

until her hands were
red raw.

The day went very
quickly.

"You'll never guess
what!" Daisy said,
rushing in from
outside just before
dusk. "I found
a vegetable
garden!"

Holly, Polly and Felicity followed her outside and round to the kitchen door, where there was a large rectangle of earth surrounded by a low wall and spotted with carrot tops, potato plants, runner beans and tomatoes.

"It was all underneath the over-growth!" she told the fairies as they returned inside.

"Oh, Eliza, why didn't you come to see?" Felicity asked, realizing they had left her indoors.

"Oh, I've seen it before. I just forgot it was there," she said, carrying on scrubbing the floor.

* * *

Before they knew it the weekend was over again, but the house was looking amazing. Winnie had repaired the outdoor staircase and cleaned all the windows, Felicity had filled in the damaged bits of wallpaper, matching the colours exactly, and the garden was looking wonderful thanks to Daisy. The wooden floorboards were shining with polish and the walls were vibrant with colour.

The fairies had washed the heavy curtains on the four-poster beds and the sheets were crisp and clean, ready to be slept in. The kitchen was filled with the smell of fresh vegetables as Daisy cooked up a feast straight from the garden, and the dining table was laid with sparkling plates and cutlery.

"You know, I don't think it will take long until we've finished," Polly said as they settled down for their evening meal.

"I'll miss you all when you've gone," Eliza said sadly.

Felicity placed a comforting arm around her shoulder.

"Don't be silly, we'll still come to see you. Where do you live, anyway?"

"Oh, just over there," Eliza replied, gesturing behind her.

"Well, we'll keep coming to visit the house. We haven't done all this work for it to get spoilt again!" Holly said, looking around.

"What exactly should we do with the house?" Polly asked.

None of the fairies had thought about it. They had just wanted to restore it to its original beauty. After that they had no idea what they were going to do!

"We could tell the estate agent in Little Blossoming it's up for sale," Holly suggested.

"But we don't know who owns it, so we can't sell it," Daisy pointed out.

"We could ask Fairy Godmother what to do," Polly said.

"Or we could turn it into a museum so that fairies from all over Fairy World could come to see our wonderful house!" Felicity said, getting excited.

"But it's not ours!" Winnie reminded her.

"I think we need to find out who owns the house first before we decide what to do with it," Polly suggested sensibly. "I'll try to find something in the library tomorrow."

* * *

The next day Polly disappeared into the library as soon as the bell went for lunch.

Felicity was sitting with Holly,

Winnie and Daisy under the Large Oak
Tree, daydreaming about the beautiful
house, when Polly came rushing up to
them all, her wings shaking.

"You'll. Never. Believe.
It," she spluttered,
trying to
catch her
breath then
signalling
for the
fairies to
follow her as she spun around and
headed back towards the library. Once
inside she showed them an old, faded
newspaper and pointed to the picture
on the front page.

Holly, Daisy, Felicity and Winnie
gasped.

"Shhh!" Miss Page, the school
librarian said. "Silence in the library."

The fairies all looked at each other,
their eyes wide open with shock.

On the page spread out in front of them was the headline, "Fairy Goes Missing. House Abandoned" with a picture of the old house underneath, beside a picture of Eliza. Polly pointed to the date in the corner of the page; it was over two hundred years old!

The fairies photocopied the front page of the newspaper and took it outside to read.

"A local fairy is mysteriously missing,"

Polly read to the others. "Eliza Besset went home from school on Friday as usual to her large house on the outskirts of Little Blossoming. When she didn't return on Monday morning her friends started to worry and called the police. Upon inspection of her house the police found all the furniture covered in dustsheets and the house completely abandoned. All of Eliza's personal belongings had been removed and she has left no note as to her whereabouts. The police are urging anyone who has any information about this young fairy to come forward immediately."

"Oh, my goodness!" Daisy whispered, shaking from her toes to the tips of her wings.

"It can't be," Felicity said, looking at the newspaper page.

"It's unbelievable," Holly said.

"We have to go back to the house,

tonight!" Winnie said at the end of lunch.

None of the fairies could concentrate in their last lesson of the day and they flew as fast as they could to the old house as soon as the last bell rang.

The door was closed but not locked and Winnie went inside, peering around each doorway looking for Eliza.

"Eliza, Eliza!" The fairies called, but there was no response. They checked every room and all around the garden but Eliza was nowhere to be seen.

The fairies left the house, wings drooping.

"Hang on, what's that?" Winnie said, bending down to the front doormat as they left. They had been in such a rush on their way in that the fairies hadn't seen the note tucked under the corner of the mat.

Felicity unfolded it to see beautiful swirly handwriting.

Dear Felicity, Winnie, Holly, Polly and Daisy,

I can't tell you how wonderful it has been working with you all to make my house look beautiful again. It broke my heart to have to close it up all those years ago and I have returned many times since then, but I just couldn't look after the house all on my own. You have made my house shine again and now I can rest in peace, knowing that you will look after it. Please enjoy my house as much as I did when I lived here.

Love, Eliza Besset

For the second time that day the fairies were all shocked.

"I'm so glad we made her happy again," Daisy said with a tear in her eye.

Felicity gave Daisy a big hug, sad that she wouldn't see Eliza again.

* * *

That night in bed, Felicity thought of all the wonderful ways she could open the house up for everyone to see. A museum was a good idea, but she wanted the beds, chairs and tables to be used, not just looked at, and the shiny floorboards and bright rugs would get ruined with fairies from everywhere trampling through. Perhaps they should use it for school, a history project or place to rest at the weekends – or they could open it as a hotel? It wasn't long before Felicity fell fast asleep, dreaming of all the possibilities the house had to offer…

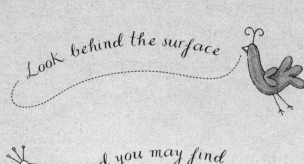

Look behind the surface

and you may find
something unexpected!

TV Triumph

"And then," said Holly enthusiastically, "she flew away and said, 'I'll be back soon, don't forget me' – and then it ended!"

Felicity Wishes was fluttering along the school corridor with her friend Holly, discussing their favourite television programme. Felicity had missed last night's episode because she was visiting the old mansion the fairies had just finished restoring. The house lay on the outskirts of Little Blossoming and had been a ruin for many years, but thanks to Felicity and her friends it now sparkled like new.

"Thank you so much for filling me in. I can't believe I missed it!" Felicity told Holly.

"That's OK. How was the house?" Holly asked.

"Just the same as usual; cold and lonely. It's such a shame to leave it empty," Felicity replied, stopping to let a group of fairies past.

Felicity tried to carry on along the corridor but Holly held her back.

"Listen!" Holly whispered, edging towards the door of their history class.

"So, you don't know of any houses that might be appropriate?" a theatrical voice boomed. Felicity instantly recognized it as Miss Glitz, the drama teacher.

"No, there are no old houses with original features in Little Blossoming. Your friend will have to go much further away to find any such thing," Miss Fossil, the history teacher, replied.

"No, she really wants to remain in Little Blossoming. She simply must find a house here," Miss Glitz said, her voice getting louder.

Just then the door opened and Felicity and Holly, who'd had their ears pressed against it, stumbled into the room.

"Oh!" Felicity gasped, as she picked herself up. "Oh, sorry, we didn't mean to, erm, eavesdrop, it's just…" she said, looking at the amused expression on Miss Glitz's face.

"Yes, yes, carry on," Miss Glitz said as Felicity's cheeks grew pinker by the second.

"We heard you asking about an old house, one in Little Blossoming. We know just the place," Holly said, helping her friend.

"We're looking after an old mansion over the hill. We've cleaned and restored it and it's got all the original features," she said, glancing at Miss Fossil.

Miss Fossil smiled. "It sounds just like what your friend wants!" she said to Miss Glitz.

"Yes, when can we go and have a look?" Miss Glitz asked the girls.

"Today, after school, if you'd like," Felicity suggested.

"Perfect. The sooner the better!" Miss Glitz bellowed, clapping her hands together.

"There's just one thing," Felicity said. "What exactly is it you want the house for?"

"Oh, didn't you hear me say?" Miss Glitz replied as she swished out the door. "My friend is a very well-known television producer. She wants to film a reality TV programme in a period house!"

* * *

Felicity and Holly rushed to their next lesson to tell Polly, Daisy and Winnie the exciting news. The rest of the day seemed to last for ever. The fairies simply couldn't wait to show Miss Glitz and her friend Kitty, the television producer, around the house.

"Oh, the garden is simply wonderful!" Miss Glitz said as the fairies fluttered through the front gates and up the

drive after school. Daisy had planted
lavender bushes and beds of all
different-coloured roses in between
the old trees bordering the long drive
leading to the mansion.

As Felicity unlocked the front door
to let Kitty and Miss Glitz into the
house, they both gasped.

"How marvellous!" Miss Glitz
exclaimed, spreading her arms out in
the huge hall. "Such a grand staircase!"

Kitty remained very quiet, but then,
as they finished the tour and arrived

back in the entrance hall, she spoke for the first time.

"Excellent! The house is exactly what we have been looking for," she said, smiling at the fairies. "Now, we need another five fairies to take part in the television show. Would you be interested?" she asked.

Felicity looked at her friends, bursting with excitement.

"Yes, please!" she replied, knowing this was an opportunity none of the fairies would want to miss.

Once Miss Glitz and Kitty had left, Felicity, Holly, Polly, Daisy and Winnie danced around the house with excitement, cheering and clapping at the thought of being on TV!

Kitty had filled them in on the programme details: ten fairies would live together in the house, exactly as the fairies who lived there a hundred years ago would have lived. They wouldn't be allowed to take anything in with them from their modern lives and had to entertain the viewers by being themselves.

For the first five days a fairy would be sent home every day. The viewers would vote on who stayed and who left. The last two days the final five fairies had to be as entertaining as possible, then the viewers would decide a winner who would be cast in a period film. It all sounded so wonderful!

"I'm not sure we can afford to miss a whole week of school though," Polly said as the fairies left the house that night. "Imagine how much catching up we'll have to do."

"It will be a fantastic experience though. You can't get a better history class than actually living history!" Winnie said.

Fairy Godmother agreed with Winnie the next day at school. "You can write a report for the school newspaper about life in the house and what it would have been like to live in the past without modern conveniences," Fairy Godmother said. "Then you can give a school assembly and tell everyone what you learnt. The experience certainly is too good to miss!"

✳ ✳ ✳

Kitty had told the fairies filming was due to start in one month, which was a very long time to wait for Felicity and her friends. They weren't allowed to tell anyone what they were doing as the television company had instructed them to keep it a secret. The day before they were going into the house the fairies were simply bursting with energy.

"It'll be like a mini-holiday without even leaving Little Blossoming!" Winnie squealed.

"I can't wait to sleep in the four-poster beds!" Felicity cried.

"I'm going to be on TV! My dream come true!" Holly sighed.

"And I can spend as much time as I want in the beautiful garden," Daisy said dreamily.

* * *

But the next day the fairies discovered that life in the house wouldn't be quite as relaxing as they thought. Firstly, they had to swap their sparkling modern wands and crowns for black, ornate

ones that were so heavy
they slowed the fairies
down when flying.

Then they had to
give up their
fashionable bright dresses
for scratchy grey frocks. And,
worst of all, they had to hand
in their mobile phones!
After introducing themselves
to the other
five fairies
taking part,
Felicity, Holly,
Polly, Daisy
and Winnie sat down
at the dining table to read a letter
containing their instructions.

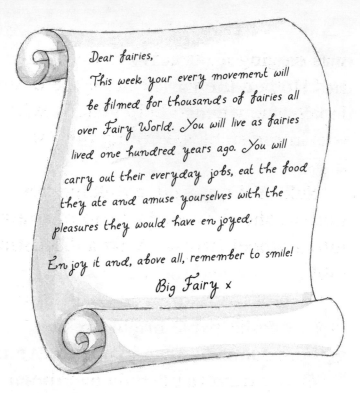

Dear fairies,

This week your every movement will be filmed for thousands of fairies all over Fairy World. You will live as fairies lived one hundred years ago. You will carry out their everyday jobs, eat the food they ate and amuse yourselves with the pleasures they would have enjoyed.

Enjoy it and, above all, remember to smile!

Big Fairy x

Next Holly read a long list of tasks the fairies had to carry out every day, taking each task in turns.

When they had allocated each fairy a job, Daisy hurriedly set off to weed the entire garden, then deadhead the flowers and cut back the bushes. She whizzed round, finishing her job in no time. Then she helped Winnie who was collecting wood for the fire, Polly who was digging up vegetables for dinner and Holly who was cleaning the house. Finally she went to help Felicity who was in the stables cleaning out the horses.

"Yuk!" Felicity said, wrinkling her nose as she shovelled a heap of straw into a wheelbarrow. "What a disgusting job!"

"It's not too bad if you talk to the horses while you do it," Daisy said, grabbing a fork and helping out.

Felicity frowned. She'd never been riding and didn't know the first thing about horses! Daisy, however, happily chatted away to the big white horse with grey spots standing over her.

When all the jobs were finally completed, the fairies got to sit back, all except Daisy who had volunteered to cook everyone supper using the vegetables she had helped Polly dig up.

Felicity, Holly, Polly, Winnie and the

five other fairies were relaxing in the
large drawing room. Felicity was trying
to remember how to play the piano,
Polly was reading a book and Winnie
was testing the walls for secret
passages.

"You know, you start to forget after

a while that you're being filmed,"
Felicity said from the piano stool.

Holly, however, had not forgotten
and was busy smiling into every vase,
candlestick and clock, just in case a
camera was hidden inside!

"Supper's ready!" Daisy called from
the dining room.

When the fairies entered they saw that Daisy had laid the table with shining silver cutlery and twinkling glasses. It looked beautiful.

"Mmmmm, it smells great, Daisy," Felicity said as she sat down.

Just then there was a loud twinkling sound like bells. It seemed to be coming from the very walls themselves! It got louder and louder until a voice boomed, "Fairies, tonight one of you must leave the mansion! The votes are in and have now been counted. In one minute we will announce who will be the first to leave the Fairy Mansion."

The voice made Daisy, who had been carrying gravy, jump into the air, spilling the gravy all over Felicity's skirt!

"Oh, no!" Felicity squealed.

"I'm sorry. I'll clear it up!" said Daisy apologetically.

"No, no. It's not the gravy. They've chosen who is going to leave. What if it's one of us?" Felicity sobbed. "I don't want to stay here without any of you!"

The fairies all looked at each other in shock. None of them had thought about leaving; they'd been so busy all day they hadn't had time.

"The fairy leaving tonight…" the voice boomed, pausing for extra emphasis, "is… Adriana!"

The fairies all heaved a sigh of relief, except Adriana, a fairy with bright-red hair, who immediately jumped up from the table with a smile on her face.

"Thank goodness!" she said. "I wouldn't have been able to last much longer without vanilla milkshake!"

* * *

The next day the fairies all swapped jobs so they could have a turn at everything. Felicity was grateful that she didn't have to clean out the horses again and instead was busy hand-washing all the curtains in the house! She had never worked so hard in her life, but she still couldn't stop thinking about the eviction at the end of the day. She couldn't bear to be parted from her friends.

At the end of the day, Felicity and her friends gathered nervously in the living room for the big announcement.

"Don't worry. Good friends are never far apart," Daisy whispered, trying to reassure Felicity.

Once again a fairy was asked to leave the mansion and, once again, it wasn't Felicity or any of her friends!

"The viewers must know that it just wouldn't be the same if one of us left!" Holly said to the others as she stood in front of a gold-framed mirror.

Daisy giggled. "I keep forgetting we're being watched. It's so much fun living here!"

Felicity pulled a face. She didn't think it had been fun. It had been far too much hard work and she really did miss her favourite pink dress.

The next three nights three other fairies were asked to leave, until only Felicity, Winnie, Polly, Holly and Daisy were left in the mansion. The fairy friends had to do more work than ever in the last two days without the other fairies around to help. When they weren't busy working they spent their time reading, singing, dancing and playing games around the big fire in the drawing room.

"I miss the library!" Polly exclaimed on their last night. "I've read all the books here. There just aren't enough!"

"I haven't found any secret passages. I can't wait to fly as far as I want without having to stop!" Winnie moaned.

"I can't believe I'm saying it, but I miss school!" Felicity laughed. "It's not as much hard work as this!"

"I just can't wait to meet my fans!" Holly said, taking a bow from an imaginary stage. "Thank you, thank you!" she called.

Daisy remained quiet.

"What's wrong?" Felicity asked her. They were playing chess on the floor in front of the fire.

"It's just," Daisy replied sadly, "I've really enjoyed being here. I don't want to leave!"

Felicity jumped up to give Daisy a big hug.

"You can come back to the mansion any time you like. It will always be here!" Felicity smiled.

"Yes, but no one else will be, and I won't have any jobs to do!" Daisy said, close to tears. All the fairies had noticed her enthusiasm during the week. She had helped everyone with their jobs, cooked supper every night and still had energy to have fun with the others.

Just then the fairies heard the familiar sound of the bells ringing in the house. The winner was about to be announced...

"It doesn't matter who wins," said Felicity over the loud bells as the fairies gathered into a circle and held hands, "we've done it together."

"The winner is…" the voice boomed, "DAISY!"

Daisy stood as still as a statue in shock, barely able to flutter her wings. Felicity, Polly and Winnie showered Daisy with hugs and Holly tried hard to hide her disappointment at not winning.

"Daisy, you have received the most votes. The public love you!" the voice continued. "You'll be starring in an upcoming film with world-class fairies and you will be famous all across Fairy World!"

Daisy had fallen into a chair in shock. For what seemed like for ever to the other fairies, Daisy sat silently, deep in thought.

"There's just one thing," she said, finally regaining her voice and looking to the ceiling as she spoke to the booming voice. "I don't want to be in the film! Can Holly be in it instead?"

There was silence.

"If you are sure this is what you want there should not be a problem with your decision," the voice eventually replied.

Holly jumped up and down as she ran to hug Daisy. "Thank you, thank you, thank you!" she sang.

Felicity giggled, truly happy that Holly's dream had come true, and truly happy that they had all lived a dream in the most beautiful house in Little Blossoming.

It's not the winning that counts

...but the taking part

Fairy Fame

Felicity Wishes and her friends were
fluttering home late on Sunday night.
They had just left the old mansion in
Little Blossoming where they had
spent the last week being filmed for a
reality television programme, living
their lives just as fairies would have
done over a hundred years ago.

"I can't wait to see everyone at
school tomorrow," Felicity said, mid-
flutter. "I've even missed cooking
classes!"

Daisy smiled. "I can't wait to see my plants. As soon as I get home I'm going straight to my greenhouse!"

"And I can't wait to start filming. It's going to be so much fun!" Holly said, doing a loop-the-loop.

Daisy had won the opportunity to star in a period film when she was voted the most entertaining fairy by the viewers of the television programme. But as Daisy didn't want to be famous and knew that it was Holly's dream to become a star, she had given Holly her prize.

The fairies parted and went to their own houses for a good night's sleep, but as Felicity fluttered towards her front door she couldn't believe her eyes. There right in front of her doorway was the biggest sack she had ever seen, brimming with letters all addressed to her! She squeezed round the side of the bag to get to

the door, but when she unlocked it and
turned the handle it simply wouldn't
open. She pushed with all her might
and eventually inched it open just
enough to peer around it, only to see
more letters piled up inside!

"Who in Fairy World are all of these from?" she asked herself as she manoeuvred a very large mauve envelope and a wand-shaped parcel. "They can't all be for me!" she said, puzzled.

But as Felicity made herself a hot chocolate and settled down in her favourite armchair to start reading some of the letters she found that they were indeed all for her, every single one!

Dear Felicity,
I loved watching you every day. My favourite bit was when you had to clean out the horse stables and you wrinkled your nose the whole time! I think you should have won.
Love Penny

The letters went on and on. Every single fairy had lovely things to say to Felicity and she simply couldn't stop reading them.

"Just one more, just one more," she told herself as every hour went by until the sun was rising and it was time to get ready for school.

Dear Felicity,
You are great! I've never met you, but it feels like you're my best friend.

Love Susie

Felicity Wishes
Little Blossoming

Felicity arrived at the school gates rather bleary-eyed, only to find it was absolutely buzzing with fairies she had never seen before. Some were holding great big cameras on their shoulders and microphones in their hands. Others had banners saying "We Love Daisy" and "Felicity is the Best!" The big crowd screamed with excitement as they spotted

Felicity approaching, and were swarming around her within seconds.

"Please can I have your autograph?" fairies were calling.

"Were you pleased when Daisy won?" one journalist shouted.

"How does it feel to be back to normal?" another yelled.

Whatever this was, it certainly wasn't normal, Felicity thought as she smiled at everyone. Unsure of where to look Felicity spun around to find Fairy Godmother standing next to her.

"Come along, Felicity," she said, taking Felicity's arm and leading her out of the crowd and into the school. "You don't want to be late for lessons!"

Fairy Godmother left Felicity in the school entrance hall, where Daisy, Polly, Holly and Winnie were waiting.

"Oh, thank goodness you got out!" Daisy said, hugging Felicity.

"Isn't it mad!" said Winnie excitedly.

Felicity was lost for words, which didn't happen very often! "There's, just, so, many," she spluttered.

"I know! We're famous!" Holly shouted with glee.

"Someone has named a garden centre after me!" Daisy said, jumping up and down.

"*Tooth Magic* want me to write my very own column in their magazine!" said Polly, her wings quivering with excitement.

"And Holiday Hideaway, the travel agents, want me to front their new advertising campaign," said Winnie happily.

Felicity smiled at her friends' good news.

"Did anyone else have any post?" she asked everyone.

Everyone had got the same as Felicity – a huge sack full of letters from adoring fans.

"However are we going to reply to them all?" Felicity asked. "There isn't enough time in Fairy World!"

"Well, I won't have time, that's for sure," said Holly. "I start filming tonight! They want to release the film quickly whilst all the media hype is surrounding us."

"Wow! That's great news, Holly," said Daisy.

"And they want me to talk at the press conference next week," Holly said a little nervously. "I haven't a clue what I am going to say though."

"Don't worry, we'll help you think of something," said Felicity reassuringly.

* * *

The rest of the day was a blur for Felicity. Every time she left a classroom there was a huddle of fairies waiting at the door to talk to her, but as much as she loved making new friends she was too tired to answer all their questions.

At break-time Felicity, Holly, Polly, Daisy and Winnie couldn't get anywhere near the Large Oak Tree where they usually sat, because a large group of fairies was crowded round it, waiting for their arrival. And at lunchtime they spent so long signing autographs that they didn't even have time to eat before the school bell went.

Felicity had never imagined they would be this famous and wasn't sure she liked all the attention. One fairy had even asked her to sign her school bag so she could keep it for ever as a reminder that she went to school with the famous Felicity!

At the end of the day the fairies all left school by the back gates, trying to avoid the even bigger group of fairies that had formed by the main gates during the day. Polly, Daisy and Winnie flew with Holly to the film studios in Bloomfield, but Felicity was simply too tired to go all that way so, after checking to make sure Holly didn't mind, she headed home for an early night.

As Felicity approached her house she saw that another large crowd of fairies had formed around her door. When they spotted her they started

shouting out questions, and Felicity
did her best to answer every one.

"Yes, no, yes, yes, maybe, definitely,
yes!" she called out around her as she
struggled to reach her front door.

"Sorry, I have to get some sleep,"
she said as she closed the door to the
babble of fairies.

Felicity went straight upstairs, straight to bed and straight to sleep. She didn't even have the energy to change into her pyjamas or take off her crown!

* * *

After a good night's sleep, Felicity fluttered into school the next day refreshed and alert. Like the day before, a large crowd of fairies had gathered at the school gates – but Felicity was rather surprised by the questions the crowd were now asking her.

"Is it true?" one fairy asked.

"How could you say such a thing about Daisy?" another called.

Felicity made her way through the crowd and flew into the school, a puzzled expression on her face.

"Has anyone been asking you strange questions?" she asked Polly as she flew into their first class.

Polly shook her head but didn't utter a word.

"Pol, what's wrong?" Felicity asked, sensing her friend's uneasiness.

Polly reached into her bag and pulled out that morning's newspaper. In big red words across the front page it said, "FELICITY ADMITS SHE IS ANGRY AT NOT WINNING TV SHOW".

Felicity couldn't believe it. "I never said that!" she shrieked. "I'm not angry at all!"

THE DAILY FLUTTER
TUESDAY JUNE 12 2007

FELICITY ADMITS SHE IS ANGRY AT NOT WINNING TV SHOW

Our sources write an exclusive report on the true feelings of a fairy to whom friendship is supposed to be the most important thing. Is it all a SHAM?!

"I know that, Felicity," Polly soothed. "But everyone else doesn't."

There wasn't time to say any more before the lesson began and Felicity didn't have a chance to catch up with Daisy, Holly and Winnie until morning break.

"I'm not angry at all. I'm happy you won," Felicity said, rushing up to Daisy.

"I know," Daisy said, catching her friend in a hug.

"What happened?" Holly asked.

"I have no idea," Felicity replied, searching her mind for where the story might have come from. "Unless..." she began.

"What?" Winnie prompted her.

"Last night when I got home there was a group of fairies on my doorstep," Felicity continued. "They kept asking questions and I just answered as many as I could before I closed the door. Maybe..."

"Maybe… someone asked if you were angry and thought you said 'yes', when you were actually replying to another question?" Polly finished.

Felicity nodded.

"I've already had five fairies telling me I shouldn't be friends with you any more," Daisy murmured.

Felicity's face fell.

"I told them you're the best friend a fairy could ever have!" Daisy continued, cheering Felicity up immediately.

"What are we going to do?" Holly asked.

"We'll have to think of something. We can't have fairies thinking Felicity is not a wonderful friend," Polly said, taking Felicity by the arm and leading her to their next lesson as the school bell rang.

* * *

For the rest of the day Felicity

received very funny looks from fairies in the corridor and no one wanted to speak to her.

"I didn't like all the attention before, but this is even worse!" said Felicity, trying hard not to get upset in front of her friends.

After school Felicity, Holly, Polly, Daisy and Winnie all flew to Sparkles, their favourite café. They aimed straight for their normal settee by the fire and immediately started to think of ways to show everyone Felicity was not angry at Daisy winning the show.

"We could write it in chalk in giant letters on the school playground!" Winnie suggested.

"What if it rains before anyone sees it?" Polly said sensibly.

"We could make a banner and tie it to the school gates," suggested Holly.

"Or we could just tell the newspaper reporter the truth," said Daisy.

"They won't listen." Felicity sobbed. "It's no use."

The fairies were just about to give up hope of ever finding a solution, when Polly suddenly had an idea that would solve all their problems!

"Holly can't think of anything to say at the press conference – so why doesn't Felicity join her to talk about their time in the mansion and, in particular, her friendship with Daisy!"

"What a great idea!" chorused Holly, Daisy and Winnie.

Felicity remained quiet. "But what if no one wants to listen to my side of the story," she thought to herself.

* * *

The fairy friends spent the entire week preparing for the press conference, all except Holly who was busy filming in an exotic location.

Polly made sure that Holly's speech was witty and interesting and that she knew the plot and the other actors inside out. Daisy and Winnie made posters brimming with photographs of Felicity and Daisy together. And Felicity knew this was her one and only chance to set the record straight about her friendship with Daisy, so spent all week trying to put down in words what she felt about it.

* * *

As the day of the press conference finally arrived, every pupil and teacher from the School of Nine Wishes was gathered in Bloomfield Studios waiting for Felicity and Holly to begin their speech. And right at the back of the hall were no fewer than three film crews with their cameras ready to record the whole thing!

"I had no idea there would be so many film crews!" Felicity whispered as she nervously peeped behind the stage curtain.

"They've come to film your real story!" Polly reassured her.

As the audience settled into the seats, Holly walked on to the stage to rapturous applause. She bowed and curtseyed, enjoying the attention, until she suddenly remembered Felicity was waiting to come on stage.

"Before I begin," Holly announced to the audience, "Felicity Wishes has a few things to say!"

The audience fell silent.

"Go on, Felicity," said Polly, Daisy and Winnie, giving her a slight nudge and eventually leading her on to the stage by hand.

Felicity stepped forward to take the microphone.

"Yes, erm, some of you may have seen the newspaper on Tuesday and, well, I'd just like to say that I'm not angry at all that Daisy won the show. In fact, I'm very pleased for her –

Daisy is one of my best friends and she deserved to win. Well, erm, it was all just a big misunderstanding."

The hall filled with whoops and cheers as Daisy gave Felicity the biggest hug and Holly took to the microphone for her speech.

* * *

When it was all over, Felicity and her friends fluttered outside to find a group of fairies in the entrance hall waiting for them.

"I knew it wasn't true!" one fairy blurted out to Felicity.

"You're too nice to be angry!" another called.

"Daisy is lucky to have you as a friend," another said as she walked past.

Felicity smiled. She could get used to lots of attention, as long as she had her friends by her side to enjoy it with her.

There are ups and downs in life

but friends make them all OK

The fairy friends are

going on a hiking holiday

to Lotolakes in

Glittering Giveaways

Tasty Trip

Felicity Wishes was very excited – she and her friends were off on holiday together! They were sitting in Sparkles, their favourite café, trying to decide where to go.

"I think we should go on a hiking holiday to Lotolakes!" Winnie said, fluttering enthusiastically. "It's not very far from here, and I've always wanted to go."

"But why there?" asked Holly. "Why not Bubble Island or Petal Mountain?"

"Because I've been to Bubble Island

and we've all been to Petal Mountain, and Lotolakes sounds like the perfect place to go hiking," Winnie replied.

"It does sound a bit boring," complained Holly.

"It may sound boring, but it's the only place in Fairy World where you can get…" Winnie paused dramatically, "Lotolakes chocolate!"

"Oh, I've heard of that!" said Felicity, suddenly jumping up. "It's supposed to be the tastiest chocolate ever made!"

"If it's that good, why can't you get it here?" Holly asked sceptically.

"Because it doesn't travel well. Apparently, anywhere outside of Lotolakes it tastes disgusting!" Felicity replied.

"So why don't they make it here?" Daisy asked.

"The recipe is a very well-kept secret. No one knows how to make it," Winnie informed her.

"Well, if I get to taste yummy chocolate and have an adventure in the wide outdoors, I'm happy!" said Daisy, smiling.

The fairies all agreed, and flew home to pack.

* * *

The next morning they met bright and early, complete with bulging backpacks and brand-new walking shoes.

The journey to Lotolakes wasn't very long. First the fairies had to get a bus from Little Blossoming to Bloomfield – they couldn't fly very far due to their heavy bags. Then they had to get a train to Misty Glen and finally another bus to Lotolakes.

"It's not far to the campsite, according to my map!" called Winnie, leading the way as they stepped off the bus.

The scenery was breathtaking. The bus had stopped by the side of a road

in what looked like the middle of
nowhere. There were no houses or
shops in sight, only miles and miles of
tall dark trees, overlooked by rolling
green hills. By the side of the road
was a trickling stream, running with
the clearest water any of the fairies
had ever seen.

"How far exactly is the campsite,
Winnie?" asked Holly.

Felicity looked around. There were
no other fairies in sight.

"We have to follow this footpath,"
said Winnie, pointing to a muddy path
winding through the next field, "then
we go over a wall, through another
field, round a lake, past a meadow and
over a bridge. There are no roads to
the campsite, so it should be nice and
quiet there!"

The fairies looked at Winnie in
wonder. Apart from the gentle trickling
of the stream, they couldn't hear

anything – or imagine anywhere quieter.

"Come on then!" called Winnie, charging over the stream and along the footpath, the other fairies following more slowly.

The friends fluttered the first part of the way, but their wings soon became tired under their heavy loads, so they all resorted to walking – except for Winnie, who was used to this kind of adventure.

"My brand-new pink boots are getting muddy!" Felicity moaned as she delicately manoeuvred a puddle. "I really hope my new dress doesn't too."

The words were no sooner out of her mouth when Felicity slipped and toppled backwards into a very muddy puddle!

"Oh no, Felicity!" Daisy ran up to her and held out her hand to help

Felicity up, only to slip over!

Holly, Polly and Winnie tried to help their friends, but they were also trying very hard not to slip over as well. Before long they were all in fits of giggles, slipping and sliding around in the mud.

"I'd love to take a picture of us now!" Holly said. "No one at school will ever believe I got mud in my hair!"

Eventually the fairies managed to get up and keep walking. But before long they were exhausted.

"How much further, Winnie?" Daisy asked droopily.

"Not far!" Winnie replied. But she'd said exactly the same thing the last time she was asked!

Finally they reached the campsite. Felicity, Polly, Holly and Daisy immediately unfastened the heavy bags from their backs and dropped them to the ground, falling on top of

them in a big heap. There were a few
other fairies setting up their tents, and
they smiled sympathetically.

"I've-never-walked-that-far!" Holly
said, panting.

"My feet hurt!" Felicity moaned. "Why
didn't I get the sensible walking shoes
Winnie recommended?"

Daisy's wings were almost touching
the ground, they were drooping so
much!

Just then Winnie came back from
the campsite shop, holding five large
chocolate bars.

"These are for you-hoo," she sang
energetically.

"I'm too tired to eat," Polly said,
closing her eyes.

"Trust me, you want to eat these!"
Winnie said, handing one to each fairy.

They peeled the wrappers back and
started nibbling their bars of chocolate.
Almost at once the fairies cheered up.

"Thish ish elishoush," Felicity said, her mouth full.

"I heel besher aleady," Holly announced as she chewed.

They finished the chocolate with incredible speed and all jumped up from the ground, full of energy.

Winnie grinned. "I told you it was the best chocolate in Fairy World!"

Read the rest of

Emma Thomson's

Felicity Wishes

Glittering Giveaways

to discover how a chocolate

bar leads the fairies to a

chocolate world!

If you enjoyed this book, why not try another of these fantastic story collections?

Designer Drama

Star Surprise

Clutter Clean-out

Newspaper Nerves

Enchanted Escape

Whispering Wishes

7 Sensational Secrets

8 Friends Forever

9 Happy Hobbies

10 Party Pickle

11 Wand Wishes

12 Dancing Dreams

13 Spooky Sleepover

14 Fashion Fiasco

15 Pink Paradise

16 Spectacular Skies

17 Dreamy Daisy

18 Perfect Polly

19 Winnie's Wonderland

20 Holly's Hideaway

21 Fairy Fun

22 Starlight Songs

23 Crowning Cure

24 Fairy Fame

felicity Wishes

Storytelling Stars

and other stories

Storytelling Stars

felicity Wishes

Perfect Ponies

and other stories

Perfect Ponies

felicity Wishes

SALE

Glittering Giveaways

and other stories

Glittering Giveaways

Look out for these five special editions

Summer Sunshine

Holiday Hullabaloo

Emma Thomson's **felicity Wishes**

With Sparkl...

Emma Thomson's **felicity Wishes**

With Sparkling colour illustrations

felicit

With colour illustrations

felici

Holiday *and*

felici

Summ *and*

Christmas Cala *and other stories*

Winter Wishe *and other stories*

Snowy Showdown

Christmas Calamity

Winter Wishes

Snowy Showdown

SEE YOUR FRIENDSHIP LETTER HERE!

Write in and tell us all about your best friend, and you could see your letter published in one of the Felicity Wishes books.

Please send in your letter, including your name and age, with a stamped self-addressed envelope to:

Felicity Wishes Friendship Competition

Hodder Children's Books, 338 Euston Road, London NW1 3BH

Australian readers should write to...
Hachette Children's Books
Level 17/207 Kent Street, Sydney, NSW 2000, Australia

New Zealand readers should write to...
Hachette Children's Books
PO Box 100-749 North Shore Mail Centre, Auckland, New Zealand

Closing date is 31st December 2007

ALL ENTRIES MUST BE SIGNED BY A PARENT OR GUARDIAN.
TO BE ELIGIBLE ENTRANTS MUST BE UNDER 13 YEARS.

For full terms and conditions visit www.felicitywishes.net/terms

Friends of Felicity

Dear Felicity,

My Best friend is Madelynne - She's the Best friend I've had at the moment. Beacause Madelynnes nice, kind, and the best at gumnastics and sometimes teaches me how to do cart-wheels, roundoffs and bend backs. We have the time of our Lifes at shcool. Madelynne and I, also

Annaleise sometimes laugh alot and enjoy our selfs. Thats why I Love having a best friend because we can tell each other our secrets.

❀ ♥ Love from Tiffany xx

WOULD YOU LIKE TO BE A FRIEND OF FELICITY?

Felicity Wishes has her very own website,
filled with lots of sparkly fairy fun and information
about Felicity Wishes and all her fairy friends.

Just visit:

www.felicitywishes.net

to find out all about
Felicity's books,
sign up to
competitions,
quizzes and
special offers.

And if you want
to show how much
you love your friends,
you can even send
them a Felicity e-card
for free. It will truly
brighten up their day!

For full terms and conditions visit www.felicitywishes.net/terms